This book is dedicated to
my late father Shahid Syed,
may Allah have mercy on his
soul, who taught me the
importance of generosity and
to always give to others,
even before they ask.

- T.S.

Prolance

www.prolancewriting.com
California, USA
©2018 Tayyaba Syed
Illustrations ©2018 Melani Putri

ISBN: 978-0-9996991-2-6
Soft cover edition

The Blessed Bananas

A Muslim Fable

Written by:

TAYYABA SYED

Illustrated by:

MELANI PUTRI

PROLANCE

On top of the highest hill, above a giant banana plant, there lived a cranky, old monkey named Rico.

He was the wealthiest of all, for **Allah**, the Most High, had truly blessed Rico with the banana plant he called home. It bore sweet, tasty bananas all year round, so Rico never had to search for food.

He refused to share his bananas with anyone and
never thanked his Creator for all his blessings.

Rico thought he deserved all the bananas,
since he had planted and grown this plant all
by himself.

Everyone in the village below knew not to come near Rico or the hill. That was *his* home, and those were *his* bananas. Every day he sat alone atop his banana plant eating bananas and tossing the peels down below, not caring about the mess.

The monkey had everything he needed: great food, a perfect home with the best view, and a beautiful surrounding breeze. Yet, Rico felt like something was still missing.

So everyday, Rico would count his bananas to make sure they were all there.

"Three hundred five, three hundred six, three hundred seven…"

As the monkey continued counting, he heard a tiny, squeaky voice from below.

"Excuse me, sir. May the Peace of **Allah** be upon you," the little voice called out.

Immediately, Rico looked around the area to see who
would dare come near him and his bananas.

"Who's there?!" he asked not seeing anyone in sight.

"Down here," spoke a little white mouse.

Rico glared down at his feet.

"Eeeek!" he shrieked. "How dare you come up here?" questioned Rico. "This is *my* home, and you are *not* allowed up here. Now shoo!"

"I'm sorry. I didn't mean to frighten you. My name is Chico. I'm new to this area and was searching for some lunch. I made *du'a* to *Allah* to help me find food, and then I saw your yummy bananas. May I have one banana pretty please?" he asked politely.

"Listen, Mouse! Leave my home right this minute, or you will be sorry!
Everyone knows no one is allowed up here. And I don't share my bananas
with anyone!"

"I...I don't know anyone here and didn't know about your rules, sir," Chico explained softly. "I won't disturb you again."

Chico was so sad. His eyes began to well up with tears. He wondered how someone could be so selfish and mean. Out of respect for the elder monkey, Chico did not say another word and sadly scurried back down.

Ya Allah. Please guide that monkey to goodness, and with that prayer, Chico quickly went down the hill.

Rico's heart was now racing with anger. That was the first time in a long time he had talked to anyone, and he was not happy about it. He realized the unwanted meeting with the mouse had made him forget his count.

"Great. I must start all over again!" he said out loud.

As Rico began counting again, a black and yellow toucan flew down behind him and rested on the opposite side of the banana plant. She was panting very hard.

"**As salaamu alaikum**," she said between breaths. "I'm Tucana. May I rest here for a few minutes?"

Rico could feel his blood boiling and quickly turned around to see who dares to come onto his property now. He walked up close to Tucana and stared at her hard.

He then leaned in close to her face and shouted, "No!"

Tucana fluttered her wings in disbelief and backed away from him.

"I didn't mean to upset you. I had been flying for a long time and just needed a break. I saw your lovely home and didn't think you'd mind. I'll just be going then. Sorry," Tucana said kindly.

Tired and hurt, she flew off while making a quiet *du'a*.

*Oh my Lord. I forgive that monkey. Oh **Allah.** Please have Your Mercy on him too.*

Rico had had enough and decided to put up signs to keep strangers off his property, and the signs definitely worked. Days went by and no one came by Rico or his home. Rico ate and ate his bananas until his tummy hurt, yet he wasn't satisfied.

"Something is still missing," he said to himself.

One afternoon, Rico finally climbed down his plant to check up on his signs when a large, gray elephant approached him.

"**As salaamu alaikum**, brother. My name is Simón," he greeted warmly in his deep voice.

Rico turned and glared up in shock at the giant creature.

"I am not your brother," Rico replied curtly. "What do you want? No one is allowed to come near me or my home! Don't you see my signs here?"

Simón was in dire need of the monkey's help and decided to ignore his rudeness. He reached out his trunk and softly nudged Rico on the shoulder.

"You are my brother in Islam," he reminded Rico. "I need your help to find my herd. I see you live on this tall banana plant on this high hill, and I was hoping you could look from above to see which way my herd went," said Simón.

Rico had heard enough. "Get off my property right this minute! You can find your own way back!"

The words spit out of Rico's mouth. He turned his back towards the elephant and started to climb back up his plant.

STAY OFF!

GO AWAY!

NO BANANAS 4 U!!

"Brother, I beg you." Simón pleaded. "Just take a minute to look for my herd, and I'll be on my way. Please, brother. Please!"

Rico ignored him and kept climbing.

In desperation, Simón began to pace back-and-forth, not noticing all the banana peels below his huge feet. Suddenly, he started to slip and quickly grabbed onto the plant's large stem with his trunk.

"Whooooaaaa!" Simón screamed, shaking the plant as he tried to get back on his feet.

Startled and scared, Rico held on from above with both hands. Bananas came crashing down just missing Simón's head, causing him to lose his balance again and to shake the plant even harder.

Rico watched with shock as one by one, the bananas rained downward.

"My bananas!" cried Rico. "Help! Someone! Help!"

However, no one came to his rescue. He then looked up to the Heavens and prayed as hard as he could.

"*Ya Allah*! *Help me as You are the only One that can save me now!*"

At the foot of the hill, Chico and Tucana happened to be resting by a watering hole. They both worriedly looked up towards the hill when they heard all the chaos.

"Do you hear that?" asked Chico. "Someone's in trouble up there!"

"Let me fly up and check," said Tucana. She quickly flew upwards to get a better view and saw the old monkey desperately hanging onto his banana plant with panic in his eyes.

"It's the old monkey!" Tucana shouted down to Chico. "He looks like he's about to fall!"

"Oh no! We have to help him!" cried Chico.

Tucana swooped down and grabbed Chico into her long beak. She then flew up again as fast as she could through the shower of bananas and leaves. They reached Rico in no time, but she couldn't talk with Chico in her mouth.

Rico immediately recognized Tucana and was relieved to see her this time.

"Please help me!" begged Rico. "That elephant is knocking down all my precious bananas!"

Chico peeked out from inside Tucana's beak. **Ya Allah.** *Please help*, he prayed silently. He then told Tucana to fly him close to the elephant's ear. Despite Simón's magnificent size, Chico knew just what to do.

"Salawaat 'alan Nabi!" he shouted into Simón's enormous ear.

Simón didn't know where the order came from, but he quickly let go of the plant and found his footing again.

"Allahumma sali 'ala Sayyidina Muhammad," he recited with a loud exhale. Then all became calm. He looked up and saw the toucan hovering above his head with a mouse in its beak. "Peace," he greeted them.

Rico slowly climbed down to the others. He started to cry at the sight of all the fallen mushy bananas.

"Why did you knock down this monkey's bananas?" Chico questioned Simón.

"I didn't mean to do that. I got separated from my herd and kindly asked this monkey to search from above, but he refused. I then slipped on his banana peels and lost my balance," Simón explained as he gasped for breaths. "I'm sorry about all your bananas." he apologized to Rico.

Chico, Tucana and Simón all stared at Rico. No one
knew how he would respond. The monkey sat on the
ground and placed his face in his hands. He realized it
was his own carelessness and selfishness that caused all
his bananas to fall. He felt bad about how he had
treated the others, and yet they still came to his
rescue. After a few minutes of silence, he stood up.

"It's not your fault," Rico finally spoke up. "I should be the one to apologize. All these years of being alone have made me selfish and ungrateful. You each did not ask me for much. I should have helped you all. Please forgive me."

Tucana let Chico climb out of her beak. "It's ok," she said. "We already forgave you, so **Allah** can forgive us one day."

Rico finally let out a radiant smile. "Please. Come up and take rest in my home," he welcomed Tucana.

He then picked up a large bunch of bananas and placed them next to Chico. "Please help yourself."

Then he climbed to the top of his home and scanned the village below. He pointed north and said, "There! I see your herd that way."

Simón looked up at Rico, happily thanked him and then went down the hill heading north.

Then Rico shouted from atop his tree, "Oh my fellow villagers! Please come and help yourself to these bananas. What's mine is yours!"

Villagers came running up the hill from all corners gathering up as many bananas as they could.

They made breads, shakes, puddings, and all types of goodies with the fruit.

The more Rico gave away, the more bananas his plant bore.

"*Alhumdullilah!* Thank you, **Allah**, for everything," Rico cried out in happiness, as he was no longer counting bananas and was finally feeling satisfied.

Nothing was missing anymore. He now enjoyed his blessed bananas atop his home with his new friends Tucana and Chico, and the best part was that the bananas tasted sweeter than ever.

The End

Allah stated: Verily Allah and His Angels send prayers upon the
Prophet: O Believers, send prayers on him and greetings (of peace).
(Qur'an 33:56)

These are the benefits one will receive through reciting
prayers and greetings (Salawāt) upon Prophet Muhammad,
peace and blessings be upon him.

Benefits of reciting Salawāt:

Allah will send 10 mercies upon the one who recites prayers once upon the Prophet ﷺ.

Allah will forgive 10 of his/her sins.

Allah will raise his/her rank 10 times.

Allah will grant him 10 rewards.

The recitation of Salawāt before du'a brings hope of its acceptance.

It will bring intercession of the Prophet ﷺ on the Day of Judgment.

It is a cause of forgiveness.

It brings the Pleasure of Allah.

It will bring the reciter nearer to the Prophet ﷺ on the Day of Judgment.

It will remove all his/her worries in this world and the Hereafter.

Excerpt from *Salāt and Salām* by Shaykh Muhammad Saleem Dhorat

Recipes

1. Tucana's Favorite: Banana Date Shake

Ingredients:

2 cups unsweetened almond milk
½ cup crushed ice
2 overripe bananas
6-8 pitted dates
2 Tbsp. flaxseed meal
¼ cup unsweetened coconut flakes
1 Tbsp. unsweetened cocoa powder (optional)
¼ cup sliced almonds (optional)

Directions:

1. Mix all ingredients in blender until smooth and creamy.
2. Top with whipped cream.
3. Enjoy!

Recipe by Tayyaba Syed

2. Rico's Favorite: Banana Nut Date Bread

Ingredients:

1 cup flour
1 tsp. baking soda
1/2 tsp. salt
2 eggs
1 stick of butter, melted
2 overripe bananas, mashed or chopped up
5-6 large pitted dates chopped up in small pieces
1/2 cup of chopped walnuts

Directions:

1. Preheat oven to 350 degrees.
2. Grease 9 x 5 loaf pan or line with parchment paper.
3. Mix all the ingredients well, pour into the pan and bake for 40 minutes or until top is brown and toothpick inserted in middle comes out clean.
4. Enjoy!

Recipe by Sofia Alam

3. Chico's Favorite: Banana Pudding

Ingredients:

2 large boxes of instant vanilla pudding
2 cups cold milk
1 cup sour cream
8oz. heavy whipping cream
2-3 large bananas
Vanilla wafer cookies

Directions:

1. Peel and slice bananas into medium-sized coins. Set aside.
2. In separate bowl, stir both boxes of pudding mixture with milk.
3. Stir in heavy whipping cream.
4. Mix in sour cream last, folding it into the pudding mix. Layer the bottom of a 9 x 13 glass dish with cookies and then sliced bananas.
5. Pour half of the pudding mix over the bananas and cookies, spreading evenly.
6. Repeat layers ending with pudding mix on top.
7. Refrigerate overnight.
8. Serve cold and enjoy!

Recipe by Mariam Masood

4. Simón's Favorite: Banana Ice Cream

Ingredients:

2 large ripe bananas

Directions:

1. Peel and slice the bananas into thick coins.
2. Place the sliced bananas into an airtight freezer bag.
3. Freeze the bananas overnight or for a minimum of 2 hours.
4. Pulse the frozen bananas in a food processor, regularly pausing to scrape down the sides with a rubber spatula, until creamy.
5. Blend a little more to aerate the ice cream.
6. Transfer into an airtight container and freeze until ice cream is solid.
7. Enjoy!

Recipe by thekitchn.com

About the Author

Tayyaba Syed is an award-winning author and freelance journalist. Her work has been featured in numerous publications like *NPR*, *Chicago Parent*, *Islamic Horizons*, *Azizah Magazine*, *Chicago Crescent*, and *Halal Consumer Magazine*. She co-authored four chapter books in the popular kids' series *Jannah Jewels* and works as the Research Specialist for Daybreak Press as well as a Curriculum Consultant for Whitestone Foundation's Author Development Program. She also designs unique plots for *Noor Kids* educational books as their Creative Developer.

Tayyaba travels extensively to share her passion for reading and writing by conducting literary seminars for all ages. She was selected to present a biographical paper on Fatima al-Fihri at Georgetown University's Writing Women's Lives Conference in Qatar. While there, she was invited as a guest lecturer at Texas A&M to teach writing to university students. Additionally, she has led a writing intensive at Zaytuna College in Berkeley, California, and even presented to aspiring writers in Istanbul, Turkey.

Tayyaba volunteers as a youth mentor and is pursuing her Islamic Studies certification through the Ribaat Academic Institute, while working on her next novel. She lives in Chicago with her husband and three children and enjoys baking sugar-free desserts in her free time.

Learn more at www.tayyabasyed.com.

About the Illustrator

Melani Putri is an illustrator based in Jakarta, Indonesia.
After finishing her visual art education at Bandung Institute
of Technology, she has been focusing on children's book
illustration and has won the National Folktale Illustration
award in 2016. Her illustration works include children's books,
greeting cards, posters and stationery.

Please visit her website at www.memels.com.

The Blessed Bananas was made possible in part by the
Whitestone Foundation Author Development Program.
www.authordevelopment.org

CPSIA information can be obtained
at www.ICGtesting.com
Printed in the USA
LVHW071703080319
609993LV00002B/8/P